®

Text by John Peel

Cover Illustration by Paul Vaccarello

Interior Illustration by John Nez

Western Publishing Company, Inc.,
Racine, Wisconsin 53404

© 1993 Brøderbund Software, Inc. All rights reserved. Printed in the U.S.A. No part of this work may be reproduced or copied in any form without written permission from the copyright owner. Where In Space Is Carmen Sandiego?® is a trademark of Brøderbund Software, Inc. All other trademarks are the property of Western Publishing Company, Inc. Library of Congress Catalog Card Number: 93-77423   ISBN: 0-307-22207-1   A MCMXCIII

Your Briefing

Congratulations — you've been hired as a rookie detective for the Acme Detective Agency. Your goal is to outsmart Carmen Sandiego and her gang by solving the cases in this book.

There are four cases to solve. Start by removing the cards from the middle of this book. Divide the cards into four groups. You should have the following:

4 Stolen Object Cards
4 Bookmark/Scorecards
8 Suspect Cards
8 Solar System Map Cards

Each case involves a stolen object. Decide which case you are going to solve by picking a **stolen object card**. Put the other stolen object cards away until you are ready to solve those cases.

Use a different **scorecard** for each case. As you read through each case, you will be given clues about the suspects. Write these clues down on your scorecard. Compare these clues to your **suspect cards.** Only one suspect will fit all the clues. Once you have picked a suspect, set aside the other cards until the next game.

Each time you are told to go to a different number in the case, mark your **scorecard**. These are your travel points.

When you go to a new number, you may use the **scorecard as a bookmark** to hold your place while you're investigating — sometimes you will have to retrace your steps.

Use the **Solar System map cards** for information about the various places that you'll have to visit while tracking down a suspect.

HOW TO SCORE THE GAME:

To win, you must solve the case by finding the right suspect in the right place. You cannot win if you capture the wrong suspect. Once you've found the crook and the stolen object, add up your **total travel points**. Check this score on the last page to see if you've earned a promotion. You earn a promotion by capturing the crook and stolen object in as few moves as possible. The lower your total number of travel points, the more chances you have of earning a promotion.

Ready? Okay — put on your raincoat and hat and get ready to blast off on another dangerous mission for the Acme Detective Agency.

It's been pretty quiet at the Acme Detective Agency since you managed to crack that last Carmen case and send the villains from her gang off to jail. You sort of miss the excitement, because it's been very dull since then. You complain about it to your secretary, but she's not very sympathetic.

"It's worse for me," she growls. "Not only do I have very little work to do, but I've also got to listen to your complaining. I wish you *would* get a job. Then *I'd* get some peace and quiet around here."

At that moment the phone rings. You snatch it fast, before your secretary can get it. It's the most exciting thing that's happened all week, and you're not going to let her have all the fun.

It's the Chief, and he orders you to report to his office. He sounds worried. You're not exactly happy that he's worried, but if he sounds like this, it must mean there's a case on the way. You hurry to his office. When you arrive, he hands you a card with an address on it.

"Get over to this place right away," he tells you, and hands you an address. "I've just received bad news about Carmen Sandiego."

"That's great," you say without thinking, but you quickly tell the Chief, "I mean, gee, that's terrible."

The Chief scowls. "She's broken out of jail, hopped a spaceship, and shot off into space somewhere," he tells you. "I've heard she's assembled a new gang — literally. Some of the gang have been assembled from scrap metal. You have four cases to look into."

You look at the address he's given you. It's for a place called GROK — the Galactic Research Operating Kernel — and a man called Saunders. You wonder if it's Kernel Saunders.

"You can pick up a fully equipped ship at GROK," the Chief says. "They've selected a Cosmohopper 911 Turbo for you. It's fueled up and ready to go. The on-board computer is a VAL 9000, top of the line. It's been programmed with all the relevant files — stolen objects, suspects, and all the information you'll need to track down the crooks. Now get going."

You nearly knock the Chief over as you rush out of his office. A Cosmohopper 911! That's supposed to be an awesome ship. It can go from zero to 6,000 miles in thirty seconds flat! You can't wait to get behind the wheel. When you reach GROK, Saunders is there. He shows you to the ship and runs through its operation. Finally he switches on VAL for you.

"Just pick which stolen object you'll go after first," he explains. "Then follow VAL's instructions."

Once he's gone, you're given the all-clear to lift off. You grin happily and start the engines.

The Cosmohopper zips into the Earth's orbit so fast that you almost leave your breakfast behind. Once you're in orbit, you ask VAL for the location of the stolen objects. Time to get started!

If you decide to go after:

Charon (the moon of Pluto) — go to #19
The Great Red Spot of Jupiter — go to #82
Halley's Comet — go to #134
The asteroid Icarus — go to #161

The Chase

#1. You've arrived on the shores of Neptune's ammonia sea. You're glad you packed your thermal underwear on this trip, because it is not swimming weather! You see what look like icebergs floating in the water, and you are near the planet's equator! You find a pointy-eared person wandering on the beach and ask him about the thief you're trailing.

"My name is Mr. Spark," the man tells you, raising a pointy eyebrow. "Logically, you are a detective. The person that you seek was indeed here and left a book — *A Fall of Moondust*, by Arthur C. Clarke, in fact. The thief remarked on the coldness here and spoke of going somewhere that was very close to the sun."

You thank him and wish him luck cleaning up the moondust. You hurry back to your ship at #163 before he can figure out what you're talking about.

#2. Callisto is Jupiter's eighth moon, and it has been described as a "dirty snowball." That's because it's a dark moon, with bright splashes that are craters. There's one huge crater, more than 1,800 miles across, called Valhalla, and it is here that you find a nightclub. It's not very busy, and you manage to talk to one of the dance instructors, an alien being with eight legs.

"It helps me to keep step . . . and step . . . and step," the creature explains. "Do you want to learn to dance? We're having a special on the Callisto Calypso this week."

"Sorry, I've got two left feet," you reply.

"That's nothing," the creature replies. "I've got *four*."

You ask the alien about the thief that you're trailing.

The creature grins . . . and grins . . . and grins. It's got three mouths, too. "Sure, the crook was here. Wouldn't take any dancing lessons, either. Said something about going to a place a hundred million miles from the Sun."

You thank the creature and leave it dancing with itself across the floor as you head back to your Cosmohopper at #82 to check out this clue.

#3. You've landed on Titan, the second-biggest moon in the Solar System. You feel like the biggest fool in the Solar System, because it's deserted. Better zip along to #66 to find out why.

#4. You arrive at a large volcano on the surface of Saturn's moon Titan. It's been belching all sorts of gases into the air, mostly methane and propane. Volcanoes like this are what make Titan's atmosphere so thick. You see somebody at the volcano with a huge suction device, trying to bottle the gases.

"It's great for barbecues," he tells you. "I can make a fortune with this stuff."

"I hope you find some customers out here," you say. You ask about the crook you're trailing.

"Oh, it was here," he tells you. "Odd-looking thing. Said something about going on to a planet with very little gravity — even less than Earth's gravity."

You thank the would-be salesman and head off back to your ship at #57 to check out your latest clue.

#5. You've arrived back on Earth! It's the only planet in the Solar System where life is known to exist. What a great planet! After the places you've been to, it sure is nice to be home.

You have time to grab a burger, fries, and a soda before VAL interrupts you.

"Yuck," VAL complains. "How can you eat that stuff?"

"Don't knock it till you've tried it," you tell her. "What have you got for me?"

"Something a lot less fattening," VAL answers. If you want to check out:

The Marianas Trench — go to #71
Mount Everest — go to #46
The Dead Sea — go to #133

If you think the crook went to:
Titan — go to #109
The Moon — go to #17
Jupiter — go to #100

#6. You've trailed Avery Littlebit Phelps to the crater on the Earth's moon named Plato, just like the famous Greek philosopher. You'd better be philosophical, too, because there's no sign of Avery. Take off for #104 to find out why.

#7. From a distance, Saturn's rings look like two rings separated by a gap (called Cassini's division, after the astronomer who first spotted it). Actually, there are thousands of rings, made up of tiny bits of rock and chunks of ice. The smallest are grains of dust, and the largest are only about the size of a family car. They all orbit Saturn like billions of little moons.

Speaking of cars, you come to a small gas station when you arrive. The sign says LAST STOP FOR 50 MILLION MILES. You ask the owner about the crook you're after.

"The thief was here," replies the owner, a weird creature that looks like a pancake with legs and arms. "Don't get many visitors, and it's very lonely. The crook said something about getting some Earth food and then heading off to a bunch of rocks somewhere in space."

You thank the creature for its help.

"No problem," it replies. "Stop by anytime. Give me a ring first, though. Ring — get it?" It laughs hysterically.

Now you can see why the creature doesn't get many customers. You head back to your Cosmohopper at #111 before it can tell you any more bad jokes.

#8. Pallas is a large lump of rock floating in space — like all of the asteroids. There's not much to see except a small boy and a large robot. As you approach, the robot starts waving its arms and yelling: "Danger! Danger! Warning, Jill Robinson! Warning, Jill Robinson!"

"I'm not dangerous," you say quickly, thinking you've scared the boy.

The boy sighs. "And I'm not Jill Robinson," he tells you. "The robot gets everything wrong."

The robot folds its arms and grumbles. "Well, you never listen to me."

You ask the boy about the crook you're after.

"Yeah, I saw the thief," he says. "Said something about going to a place with no atmosphere."

"I warned him about the crook, too," the robot says. "But would he listen? Does he ever listen?"

You're not listening — you're heading back to your ship at #161 to check out this clue.

#9. The methane waterfall on Saturn's moon Titan is quite a lovely spot. The liquid cascades down over the rocks and flows off to join the methane sea a couple of miles away. Just the sort of place to spend a honeymoon, you think, if you like *really* cold baths! There's not much else to do here, so you head back to your Cosmohopper at #109 to check out one of your other leads.

#10. The Orionids are a bunch of meteors that appear around the constellation Orion on October 21 each year. The Orionids are debris left by Halley's Comet, and on a good night, Earth-based observers can see as many as twenty-five of them. Right now, you're happy to settle for seeing one — and this one has a grumpy-looking alien holding on to it. The alien has a beard, a bumpy forehead, and a terrible scowl. You ask it about the crook you're after.

"Don't bother me," it growls. "I'm a Cling-On! And I'm in a bad mood."

What a grouch! You leave it holding on to its meteor and head back to check on another lead at #168.

#11. Chao Meng Fu is a large crater very close to Mercury's north pole. You find a small yellow car parked inside the crater. Inside the car are two strange-looking creatures. One is a white mouse wearing an eye patch, and the other is a scruffy-looking hamster.

"Hello," says the mouse cheerfully. "I'm Stranger Mouse, and this is my assistant, Pun-Filled."

"Oh, crumbs," mutters the hamster.

You ask about the crook you're trailing.

"Well," the mouse tells you, "I'm trailing a different crook myself. But I can tell you that the woman you're after left here and headed past the Asteroid Belt."

"I could use an asteroid belt," the hamster adds. "To keep my asteroid pants from falling down."

"Be quiet, Pun-Filled," says the mouse.

You leave the daffy duo and head back to your Cosmohopper at #73 to check out this new information.

#12. You've trailed Bea Miupscotti to the Diana Chasma on Venus. This is a deep gash in the ground in Aphrodite Terra. Speaking of terror, you're just a bit upset to discover no sign of Bea. Better transport over to #104 for the reason.

#13. Mozart is a fairly large crater near Mercury's equator. You discover a man there trying to erase graffiti. Somebody spray-painted the words MARIA MITCHELL IS THE GREATEST! in neon-green paint. Wow — a vandal who likes astronomers! (Maria Mitchell [1818-1889] was a great astronomer who discovered a comet in 1847.) You ask the man if he's seen the crook you're chasing.

"And who do you think did this?" he grumbles, pointing at the slogan. "Cleared out just as I was arriving. Said something about going to a planet whose gravity was greater than the Earth's."

You wish him luck with his paint removal, then head back to your ship at #75 to check out these clues.

#14. Your Cosmohopper lands you on the Moon. It's the Earth's only moon, and it's covered with craters and mountains. It looks desolate, but it's a great place to hide out. Since the Moon keeps one face permanently turned toward the Earth, the far side of the Moon is hidden from view. That side wasn't seen at all until the Russians launched a probe called Luna 3, in 1959.

"It looks like the end of the trail, partner," VAL tells you. "I've scanned the place and the crook we're after is still here somewhere."

If you want to check out:

Fra Mauro — go to #159
The Sea of Storms — go to #51
The Sea of Serenity — go to #118

#15. You've landed on Venus. The atmosphere here is very thick. It's like being in a heavy fog. In fact, you *are* in a heavy fog, and there's no sign of anyone here. Blast off to #66 to find out why.

#16. Nereid is a tiny moon of Neptune that's only 186 miles across, so it's not hard to check out the place quickly. The only interesting thing you find is a large blue box with a light on top and a sign that reads THE DOCTOR IS IN. As you study the box, a teddy bear in a long scarf pops out and grins at you.

"How do you do?" it asks. "I'm Dr. Pooh!" When you ask about the crook you're looking for, the teddy bear grins again. "I saw the crook, who mentioned going on to a place that orbits a planet."

"What did the crook look like?" you ask.

"No idea," Dr. Pooh replies. "But the fiend was reading a book, *The Island of Dr. Moreau*, by H. G. Wells. Seemed to be enjoying it."

You thank the doctor and head back to your ship at #103 to check on these clues.

#17. You've landed on the Moon. There's no atmosphere here and no sign of the crook you're tracking. Better zip over to #66 to find out why!

#18. You've reached Titan, the great moon of Saturn, which is hidden under thick clouds of gas. You're in the dark yourself, because there's no sign of the villain you're after. Beam over to #66 and you'll see why.

#19. Your Cosmohopper touches down on the cold, dismal surface of Pluto, the farthest planet yet discovered from the Sun. The warmest days here are almost 400 degrees below zero Fahrenheit. That's cold! The Sun is so small, it looks just like a bright star and casts very little light. It's not hard to see why this planet was named after the Greek god who ruled the Underworld!

Your computer, VAL, finishes scanning. "Well," she tells you, "I've got some good news and some bad news. Let's start with the bad news. The crook we're after left the planet. He, she, or it may have gone to one of three destinations. The good news is that the thief stopped at three places while on Pluto, so if you check them out, you might find a clue as to which destination is correct."

If you want to investigate:
The methane iceberg — *go to #125*
The mountains — *go to #58*
The north pole — *go to #34*

If you think that the crook went to:
The Asteroid Belt — *go to #96*
Venus — *go to #167*
Mercury — *go to #75*

#20. You've tailed Hanover Fist to the north polar cap of Mars. This grows and shrinks with the change in seasons, and right now it's pretty small. You feel pretty small yourself, because there's no sign of Hanover here. Zip on over to #104 to see why.

#21. You reach the crater Copernicus on Earth's Moon. The crater is 57 miles across, and easy to find because of bright lines leading from it that are called *rays*. It was formed quite recently — within the last couple of million years! In the crater you meet up with two robots. One is gold-colored, tall, and shaped like a man. The other robot is short and looks like a garbage can on wheels. The gold-colored one is crying, and you ask why.

"I'm C-Weepie-O," it explains between sobs. "This is my friend, U2-R1."

"Well, it's nice to be your friend, too," you reply, touched.

"No, I don't mean *you, too, are one*," C-Weepie-O says. "Everyone makes that mistake. That's why I'm crying."

You're not going to get a lot of sense out of these two! You ask about the crook you're looking for.

Between sobs, C-Weepie-O replies, "The thief

and I had an argument about who was the greatest astronomer of all time. That idiot said it was Maria Mitchell! I know it was really Percival Lowell. The crook got annoyed and shot off to some place with less than ten moons."

You leave the robot sobbing and head back to your Cosmohopper at #83 to check out these clues!

#22. The Great Dark Spot of Neptune is very much like the Great Red Spot of Jupiter — both of them are huge, swirling storms. You wish you'd brought an umbrella. The Great Dark Spot is about the size of the Earth, which makes it quite a storm! It takes seventeen days to spin around, and has lasted for years. When you land, you find a green-colored alien creature, looking very depressed. You ask it what's wrong.

"I'm a weather forecaster," it tells you. "Or, rather, an *ex*–weather forecaster. I always predicted rain, and it always *does* rain. They said they could figure that out on their own, so they fired me."

You sympathize with the creature, then ask if it's seen the crook you're chasing.

"Yeah," it replies. "I saw the thief, reading a copy of Arthur C. Clarke's *The Fountains of Paradise*. The crook mentioned something about heading somewhere, but not another planet."

You thank the creature and wish it luck finding a new job. Then you hurry back to your ship at #163 to check out these clues.

#23. The rings around Uranus are very much like the more famous rings around Saturn. There are eleven of them, and they are very faint. You find a balding man there in a spaceship.

"My name is Captain Placard, of the starship *Undersized,*" he tells you.

You introduce yourself and ask about the criminal you're tailing.

"I picked up a message from that person," he tells you. "Something about going somewhere that's smaller than a planet. Are you going after the villain?"

"Right away," you reply.

"Make it so," says Captain Placard, so you zip back to your ship at #114.

#24. Europa is a strange moon of Jupiter, with a smooth and shiny surface. As you get closer, you see that it's actually covered with ice. There are cracks and patterns all over it, some of them miles long, so it looks like a dirty snowball. You find a tall young man in a long robe there, practicing with a glowing light sword. He introduces himself as Fluke Skysquawker. You ask about the crook you're seeking.

"She was here," Fluke replies. "Said she had to stretch her legs, so we went for a walk. She mentioned that she was going on to someplace smaller than the Earth. Then she tried to steal my sword! Of course I wouldn't let her."

You thank him for his help and rush back to your Cosmohopper at #152 to check out these clues.

#25. You've landed on Mars, named after the Greek god of war because of its blood-red color. You're red, too, but with embarrassment. There's nobody here, so you blast off again and head for #66.

#26. Apollo was named after the Greek god of the Sun. Since this Sun-skimmer gets closer to the Sun than the Earth does, Apollo seems to be a perfect name for it. As you approach the strangely shaped lump of rock, you see a purple-colored creature stretched out on it, wearing sunglasses.

"Just catching some rays, man," the alien tells you.

You ask it about the crook you're looking for.

"I spotted the dude, dude," the alien replies. "Said something about going to a place where the temperature rises above zero."

You say thanks — and wonder what color the creature would be without a tan! You head back to #92 to check out this new lead.

#27. You've landed on Earth. This is one planet where there are plenty of people — too many, in fact! There's no sign of the crook, so you'd better whiz along to #66 and find out why.

#28. Lowell turns out to be a large crater on the southwestern part of Mars. As you land, you spot a small pyramid in the middle. You're about to climb to the top for a better look, when a large eye opens in the side of the pyramid and stares at you. It's not a stone pyramid, but an alien creature shaped like a pyramid.

"You step on me," it warns you, "and I'll step on *you*. And I'm much heavier than you are!" It stands up on ten thick legs to show you what it means. Underneath it is a dazed-looking blue alien fuzzball. "This is the last one who tried it."

You stare at the hairy creature, and it looks awfully familiar. Then you remember seeing it on a wanted poster! It might be one of Carmen's gang. . . . You drag the hairball out. Sure enough, in one of its six hands there's a sheet of paper — listing the addresses of each gang member!

If you're after:

Morton U. Bargandfore — *go to #40*
Kit Incaboodle — *go to #102*
Astro Fizzix — *go to #169*
Avery Littlebit Phelps — *go to #56*
Carmen Sandiego — *go to #127*
Infinity McMath — *go to #144*
Hanover Fist — *go to # 20*
Bea Miupscotti — *go to #86*

#29. Uranus was the very first planet to be discovered by an astronomer. Sir William Herschel first spotted it as a new planet in 1781, and he wanted to call it George, after the king of England at the time. You're glad he didn't — a planet named George would certainly sound a little bit silly!

VAL sighs. "While you've been sight-seeing," she complains, "I've been doing all the work, as usual. Oh, well, nobody appreciates a computer."

"Just give me the facts," you tell her, used to her complaints. "Then I can do *my* work."

If you want to check out:

☞

Ariel — *go to #65*
Titania — *go to #116*
Oberon — *go to #149*

If you think the thief flew off to:
Mars — *go to #25*
Venus — *go to #37*
Mercury — *go to #99*

#30. You've landed on Mimas, one of Saturn's moons. It was discovered by Sir William Herschel (who also discovered the planet Uranus). The only thing you discover is that Bea Miupscotti isn't here. You'd better zip off to #104 right away.

#31. Phobos is the moon closest to Mars, and it looks like a lump of rock about 17 miles across. There are a couple of really large craters on it, and in one crater you see a small scarlet alien creature. It must be a Red Dwarf. You ask it if it's seen the crook you're chasing.

"Yes," it squeaks. "Said something about going to look for water. Dropped this as the ship left." It hands you a dog-eared copy of *The Invisible Man*, by H. G. Wells.

You thank the dwarf and head back to the Cosmohopper at #106 to check out these clues.

#32. Homer is a fairly large crater on Mercury's equator. You discover several large billboards stuck in it. One reads HOMER: THE RANGE. Another says VISIT THE EQUATOR CRATER. You spot a small yellow alien hammering another sign in and say hello.

"Hi," the alien replies. "I'm Tessa, from a race called the Times. And these are the signs of the Times."

You groan at this terrible pun and ask about the villain you're seeking.

"She was here, but there's no *sign* of her now." Tessa laughs. "She went to a place where there are a lot of moons." As the little creature hammers away, one of the tacks splits in two. "Darn. I just broke a nail."

"Later, crater," you say to Tessa and beat a hasty retreat to your ship at #73 before either of you can come up with any more bad jokes.

#33. You've trailed Carmen Sandiego to the Maxwell Mountains located on Venus, which are over 35,000 feet high — a fifth taller than Mount Everest. You may as well rest for a while, because she isn't here. Then beam over to #104 to find out why.

#34. You've reached the north pole of Pluto, the coldest place on the coldest planet in the galaxy. There you find an ice cream stand, owned by a huge green alien wearing armor.

"I'm an Ice Worrier," it tells you. "And I'm *very* worried about my business. I don't seem to be getting many customers."

"Maybe you'd do better selling *hot* dogs," you suggest. Then you ask about the thief you're tracking.

"I saw the crook. Said something about going to a place that was closer to the Sun than the Earth."

You thank the owner. "Think about the hot dogs," you add, and then you head back to your ship at #19 to check out your clue.

#35. Jules Verne is a large crater on the dark side of the Moon. It's completely hidden from anyone on Earth — but not from your Cosmohopper! As you fly over, you spot Hanover Fist lurking in the bottom of the crater.

Thinking fast, you put your ship under control of VAL. "Bring us in close," you instruct her. You attach a hose to the water tank, and as you fly over Hanover, you spray him with water. In the chill of the Moon, this instantly turns into ice, trapping him nicely.

"One villain on ice," you say with a grin. "Okay, VAL, contact the Chief." When the Chief appears on the viewscreen, you report that you've caught Hanover Fist and that he's ready to confess where he's hidden the Great Red Spot.

"Great work," the Chief replies. "Well, I'll have the police drop him off at the Jailhouse Rock. You'd better head for the back of the book and see if you've earned that promotion!"

#36. The Comet West appeared in 1976. It is now out and away from the Earth again, and when you view it, it looks like a rocky ball of ice peacefully floating in space. Talk about the not-so-wild West! You see an alien creature dressed in a maid's uniform, dusting off the comet.

"There's so much dust on these comets," the creature complains. "It takes forever to keep them clean!"

You ask about the crook you're after.

"Oh, that person was here, trailing mud all over my nice, clean comet. I said it would take forever to wax. The villain replied that there was lots of ammonia on the next stop of the getaway, and promised to send me some. I wonder how long it will take to get here."

"Forever," you reply — and hurry back to your ship at #134 to check out this clue before you're asked to help polish the rocks!

#37. Your Cosmohopper slows down as it enters the thick atmosphere of Venus. It's impossible to see anything at all through the fog, so you switch over to radar. The thick atmosphere has helped to raise the temperature on Venus, so that it's hot enough here to melt lead!

"You really lucked out this time," VAL informs you. "According to the sensors, the crook's ship is still here. I can't quite be sure where, but it's in one of three spots."

If you want to investigate:

Ishtar Terra — go to #61
Aphrodite Terra — go to #153
Beta Regio — go to #95

#38. The Caloris Basin on Mercury is 800 miles wide and surrounded by mountains, many of which are over a mile high. In the middle of it is an alien-looking gymnasium. There's a very muscular creature there, pumping iron with three sets of arms. On the wall is a sign: BURN OFF CALORIES IN CALORIS.

"Have you come to work out?" asks the creature.

"Just to work out clues," you reply. You explain you're tracking a thief.

"I saw the thief," the weight lifter tells you. "Talked about going to a place where the temperature was colder than three hundred below. I told the thief to bundle up."

"Good idea," you say, then set off to your ship at #75 to check out this clue — and to make sure you packed an extra sweater!

#39. You've reached Mercury, the planet closest to the Sun. But that's all you're close to!

There's no sign of the crook you want. Better shoot over to #66 to see why.

#40. You've trailed Morton U. Bargandfore to a huge red plain on Mars named Hellas. Alas, he's not there. You may as well pack it in and get over to #104 next.

#41. Proteus is a very small moon close to Neptune. It's hardly more than a ball of rock. When you land, you see a couple of bright orange alien fuzzballs bouncing around. You ask them if they've seen the villain you're after.

"Oh, sure," bleeps one of them. You can't tell which, since they're both bouncing up and down and you can't see a mouth under all the hair. "Spoke about setting up a methane mine on the next stop. Was reading *The War in the Air*, by H. G. Wells."

You thank them both and leave them to their bouncing games. Time to head back to your Cosmohopper at #103 to check out these clues!

#42. Rhea is the second largest of Saturn's moons, a rocky ball with ice on parts of it — and very far from Kit Incaboodle. Better roll along to #104 to see why.

#43. Hathor Mons is a fairly large mountain in the southern hemisphere of Venus. When you arrive, you see a chubby man in a kilt fixing a spaceship. You ask him how he's doing.

"Och, the engines canna take any more of this," he replies. He introduces himself as Spotty. You ask him about the crook you're trailing. "Oh, that villain was here and talked about going on to a place ninety-three million miles from the Sun. We had a wee talk about astronomers, and that scoundrel said that Galileo was the greatest ever! Can you believe it? You canna change the laws of physics, and you canna change the opinion of a daft crook."

You leave him muttering to himself about how long it will take to repair his ship, and you head back to your own at #59 to check out these leads.

#44. The Cosmohopper slows down close to Jupiter. You're approaching the asteroid group called Trojans and Greeks. These are two groups of asteroids named after the two sides that fought in the Trojan War. They're all pretty small lumps of rock, so it's difficult to know where to begin. You ask VAL how she's doing.

"Very well, thank you," she replies. "Not only that, but I've dug up some information for you.

You can give me a bonus later."

If you want to look over:

Hektor — go to #81

Achilles — go to #52

Patroclus — go to #165

If you think the crook went to:

Venus — go to #15

Mercury — go to #73

Saturn — go to #131

#45. You've tracked Astro Fizzix to the Guinivere Plain on Venus. If there's one thing that's plain, though, it's that Astro's not here. Better shoot on over to #104 to see why.

#46. The Cosmohopper lands at the peak of Mount Everest, the highest spot on Earth at 29,000 feet. It was first climbed in 1953. You find a small café there, run by Tibetan monks. As you go over to talk to the manager, he hands you a bowl of chips. He must be the chip monk. You ask about the crook you're after.

"Yes, it was here," he replies. "Mentioned something about going off to take a methane bath to wash out its circuits."

You thank him for his help. Still munching chips, you head back to your Cosmohopper at

#5 to check out these leads.

#47. Io is the innermost of Jupiter's moons, and a fascinating place. It's the only other globe in the Solar System where active volcanoes have been spotted. You see a few of them belching out flames and sulfur fumes, in fact. The surface is all red and yellow, and it looks incredibly hot down there. Then you spot seven short men, carrying shovels and picks. They're on their way to a mine, and singing: "Io, Io, it's off to work we go . . ."

You ask them if they've seen the crook you're chasing.

"Yes," says their leader. "The thief was trying to get into our diamond mine." He glares at you suspiciously. "You trying to steal our diamonds, too?"

"No," you answer. "I'm trying to catch that crook. Any help you can give me will make my job easier."

"Can't be harder than mining," the dwarf grumbles. "But I do recall some mention of going on to a planet with more than a dozen moons."

You thank them all and head back to your Cosmohopper at #82 to check out this clue.

#48. You've reached Jupiter, the largest planet in the Solar System. You've also made a large mistake, because there's nobody here. Better move on to #66 right away.

#49. You've landed on Saturn's moon, Titan, which is named for mythical giants of Greek history. This path is also history, so you'd better streak on to #66.

#50. You've reached the Asteroid Belt, which is just a bunch of rocks in space. You feel dumber than a bunch of rocks yourself, because there's nothing here. Head on to #66 and you'll see why.

#51. Despite its name, the Sea of Storms is as quiet as every other place on the Earth's Moon. This "sea," like all the others on the Moon, hasn't been liquid for 3 billion years or so. And then it was molten lava, not water! There no sign of anyone here, though, so you'd better head back to #14 and try a different lead. Better luck next time!

#52. Achilles is one of the Greek asteroids of the planet Jupiter. It's only a rock floating through space, but there is a small shopping mall on the surface. The only store open is a health food store, and a strange-looking orange snakelike thing sits behind the counter. You ask it if it has seen the crook you're trailing.

"Sssure," hisses the alien. "Sssaid wasss going sssomewhere with low gravity. Bessst way to loossse weight!"

You thank it for the clue and head back to your ship at #44 to look into this lead.

#53. The Sea of Tranquillity on Earth's Moon is a large plain where the first humans landed. Neil Armstrong and Buzz Aldrin stepped out onto the lunar surface here on July 20, 1969. Now the spot is occupied by a used-spaceship lot. The owner is a greenish creature with a big smile on both its mouths, comes over to shake your hand. It's got several of its own.

"Welcome to Honest Fred's," it says, beaming. "Best place to buy a spaceship in the Solar System." Fred points at an old Apollo landing module. "How about that beauty? Only had one owner, just like new."

"I've got a nice ship, thank you," you reply. "I'm here to catch a crook."

The owner looks startled. "Look, I don't care what you've heard, once the contracts are signed, it's a deal."

"No, I'm not after you," you explain.

"Oh, you mean the nutcase that bought one of my 'Maria Mitchell Is the Greatest!' stickers," Fred replies. "Said something about going to get helium."

"That's the one," you agree.

"Never saw the crook." The creature shakes its heads.

Sure. And all its ships are good buys, too! "Good-bye," you say as you head back to your Cosmohopper at #83 to check out the clues that Fred claims not to have given you!

#54. You've reached Saturn, with its beautiful rings. Speaking of rings, your phone does. It's the Chief, ordering you to fly straight to #66.

#55. Umbriel is a moon of Uranus. It's a dark ball about 740 miles across, made up mostly of ice. You find a twenty-four-hour market there, with a big sign advertising KOOKY KOLA and a furry brown alien selling ice-cold drinks. Plenty of ice here, at least! You ask about the crook you're tracking.

"Yup, the thief was here. Tried to rob my food machine of some fresh, delicious toxic waste. You want some?"

"No thanks," you reply. "I'm trying to cut down on my toxic waste intake. Any idea where the crook was off to?"

The soda salesman shrugs. "Somewhere that's passing close to Earth."

You say thanks and hurry back to your ship at #114 to check this clue further.

#56. Syrtis Major is a big triangular-shaped area on Mars that's fringed with mountains. You've trailed Avery Littlebit Phelps here, but it's a major disappointment. Better zip along to #104 to discover why.

#57. Saturn's moon Titan is the second-largest moon in the Solar System, and it is bigger than both Mercury and Pluto! It was thought to be the largest moon, but then its orange-colored "surface" was discovered to be a cloudy atmosphere, made up mostly of nitrogen. There's a lot of methane, too, which is either liquid or ice on this moon.

While you're coming in for a landing under all this gloom, VAL finishes scanning. "You don't know how lucky you are to have me," she tells you. "If I weren't able to fish up all these leads for you, you might have to do some real detective work."

"Stop complaining," you tell her. "If you weren't working for me, *you* might be working out the value of pi to the last decimal place. Now, let me have the facts." 🖝

If you want to check out:

The methane lake — go to #87
The ice continent — go to #128
The volcano — go to #4

If you think the crook went to:
Uranus — go to #29
Neptune — go to #157
Pluto — go to #74

#58. You reach Pluto's mountains. They are cold and dark. Only an idiot would be out in a place like this. And sure enough, you spot the idiot ahead of you. It looks like a large wind-up toy robot.

Amazed, you ask, "What are you doing here?"

"Feeling depressed," the robot answers. "This is the most depressing place I've ever been."

"You should come to work with me on Monday mornings," you tell the robot, who introduces itself as Mervin.

"I'm thinking about climbing up these mountains and jumping off a cliff. But I probably won't do it. I never do anything fun."

Before Mervin does anything drastic, you ask about the crook you're chasing.

"Yes, the villain was here," Mervin says with a sigh. "Crooks depress me." You wonder why this news doesn't surprise you. "I believe the thief went on to a place with no atmosphere." The robot sighs again. "Sounds very depressing to me."

You head back #19 before Mervin gets you depressed enough to jump off a cliff yourself!

#59. Venus was once thought to be a world filled with oceans and steaming jungles. It's actually a world where the greenhouse effect has gone mad. The atmosphere is almost all carbon dioxide, and there are "rains" of sulfuric acid! The atmospheric pressure is a hundred times that of the Earth, and the temperature is over 800 degrees Fahrenheit — on a cold day! If it weren't for your special spacesuit, you'd be flattened like a pancake, melted down, and eaten up by acid. You make a mental note not to spend your next vacation here.

"Enjoying the sights?" asks VAL sarcastically. "Some of us around here work, you know."

"I'm thrilled for you," you reply. "So, what have you got?"

"A brain a million times larger than yours," VAL shoots back. "And some suggestions as to where to look.'

If you want to investigate:
Hathor Mons — go to #43
Freyja Montes — go to #155
Maat Mons — go to #101

☞

If you think that the crook's fled to:
The Moon — go to #14
Mercury — go to #76
Earth — go to #139

#60. You've arrived on Mars, the Red Planet. The soil here really is red, due to iron oxide — better known as rust! Perhaps they should call it the Rusty Planet. The planet was once thought to be the home of intelligent Martians because of an error in translation. The Italian astronomer Giovanni Schiaparelli reported in 1877 that he'd seen *canali* on Mars. The word means "channels," but it was translated into English as "canals." People thought he'd seen evidence of a civilization capable of building cities and canals! It took a long time for this idea to die down.

VAL chirps up as you land. "Well, you may not be the world's greatest detective, but you can't be *too* bad," she tells you. "My sensors indicate that the crook you're after is somewhere on this planet. The trouble is, there's a dust storm coming and I can't be certain where the villain is hiding. Over to you now, boss."

If you want to search:
Slipher — go to #136
Lowell — go to #28
Bond — go to #156

#61. Ishtar Terra is a huge continent in the north part of Venus. It contains the largest mountains on the planet, as well as a huge plateau. It's awesome! As you fly over it very low in your Cosmohopper, you spot a robot walking along. It's got seven arms, and each of them appears to have a thumb up, as if it's hitching a ride. You stop by to question the robot.

"My ship broke down over Syrtis Major," it says. "Can you give me a ride?"

"Syrtis Major?" you growl. "That's on *Mars*, dum-dum, not Venus!" You grab your laser gun. "Hands in the air!"

The robot throws up all seven hands. In one of them you notice a small computer pad. You snatch it from the robot. It's a memo from Carmen Sandiego! This must be one of her hench-things! You scan the pad with growing excitement — it's a list of all the hideouts on the planet used by her gang!

If the crook you want to arrest is:

Carmen Sandiego — go to #33
Infinity McMath — go to #108
Bea Miupscotti — go to #12
Hanover Fist — go to #141
Avery Littlebit Phelps — go to #78
Kit Incaboodle — go to #166
Morton U. Bargandfore — go to #132
Astro Fizzix — go to #45

#62. You've arrived on Pluto, the outermost planet in the Solar System. The trail's as cold as the planet is. Better head to #66 to discover why.

#63. The Perseids are a shower of meteors in the constellation of Perseus. They appear around August 11 and are actually wreckage from the comet Swift-Tuttle. Sometimes as many as fifty every hour can be seen by watchers on Earth. As you approach the Perseids, you see another spaceship among the meteors. In it is someone in a dark suit of armor, his face enclosed in a black helmet. He's breathing very heavily.

"Who are you?" you ask him.

"I'm Bath Avoider," he hisses. "The Very Dark Lord of the Sith."

"Why are you breathing so loudly?" you ask.

"Do you have any idea what I smell like?" he growls.

Boy, are you glad stenches can't travel through space! You ask him about the crook you're chasing.

"Go away!" he yells. "Baths aren't the only things I avoid. I also avoid detectives!"

You see on your calendar that it's almost August 11. "Well, I predict you'll be caught in a shower soon," you tell him. "A meteor shower!"

Then you head back to base at #168 to check out a sweeter-smelling lead.

#64. You've reached Pluto, as far from the Sun as you can get. It's also as far from any leads. You'd better take a quick trip to #66!

#65. Ariel, a moon of the planet Uranus, is covered with immense glaciers of water ice and methane ice. Unlike most moons, it does not have a lot of craters. When you arrive, you discover a red crab on a rock, singing a calypso song, "Under de Sea." He grins as you arrive.

"Hey, mon, good to see you. I'm Sub-bastian. You here to jam wit' me an' me friends?"

"No," you reply. "I'm looking for traces of a crook."

"Oh, it was here," Sub-bastian tells you. "It came to borrow a six-pack of liquid hydrogen and said it was off to get itself some nitrogen next."

You thank him for his help and ask what he's doing here.

"Waitin' for me friend," he replies cheerily. "You can always find me wit' Ariel."

That figures. Time for you to head back to your ship at #29 to check out these clues!

#66. Well, by the look of things, you've fallen for one of Carmen's tricks. You're lost, and no where near where you're supposed to be. Better retrace your steps there. You did remember to leave your scorecard there as a bookmark, didn't you? Check out the clues again and see if you can get your destination right!

#67. Iapetus is one of Saturn's moons and has a mystery. One side is normal, but the other side is covered with some dark, unknown substance. Another mystery is that there's absolutely no sign of Avery Littlebit Phelps here. Better patch out to #104 to find out why!

#68. Ganymede is the largest moon in the whole Solar System. It's 3,278 miles across, with a silicon core. Over this is an ocean about 400 miles deep. On top of that is a crust of ice 60 miles thick! You'd hate to try to go fishing here.

You spot another spaceship as you arrive. It looks like a flying saucer and has a name — *Jupiter 2* — on the side. You can see there's a whole family from the Earth inside it. You ask them if they've seen the thief you're after.

"It's no good asking us," the father replies. "We're 'Lost in Space.'"

You give him a spare map, then head back

to Jupiter at #82 to see if one of your other leads is any better.

#69. You're in the Asteroid Belt, a huge collection of floating rocks. You feel like you must have rocks in your head, because there's no sign of your quarry. Better head to #66 to find out why.

#70. Mars is dead ahead, but you must be dead in your head, because there's nobody here. Blast off for #66 right away!

#71. The Marianas Trench is the deepest spot anywhere in the Earth's ocean. You find it in the Pacific Ocean, and at 1,500 miles long, up to 40 miles wide, and more than 36,000 feet deep, it's not hard to find. It is deeper than Mount Everest is tall!

"Just the place to find some low life," you joke.

"Almost as low as your IQ," VAL quips back.

You spot a submarine down here, making a voyage to the bottom of the sea. You ask the captain if he's seen the crook you're after.

"It was down here," he tells you. "We found it hiding in the air shafts of our sub, so we shot it out of the torpedo tube. It said something about going into orbit around a planet."

You thank him for his help and head back to

base at #5 to check out these clues. As you leave, the submarine hits the seabed with a crunch. Ouch!

#72. You've trailed Morton U. Bargandfore to the Sea of Crises on the Earth's Moon. The sea's not the only one with problems — there's no sign of Morton here. You'd better zip off to #104 right away.

#73. Mercury is the planet closest to the Sun, and it looks a lot like the Moon does — all covered with craters. Because it has no atmosphere, the side of the planet facing the sun gets to over 600 degrees Fahrenheit, while the other side may be as low as 350 at the same moment! Though the second-smallest planet, it was seen by the earliest human observers.

As you come in for a landing, VAL tells you she's finishing scanning the planet. "It's kind of dull," she tells you. "You'll love it."

"Thanks," you reply. "Now, how about some real information?"

If you want to investigate:

Chao Meng Fu — go to #11

Homer — go to #32

Haystack Valley — go to #140

If you think the crook has gone to:
Mars — go to #77
Jupiter — go to #152
Pluto — go to #64

#74. You've reached Pluto, which is a shame, because the crook you're chasing hasn't. Zip on to #66 pronto.

#75. Mercury was one of the planets known to ancient astronomers, but not very much was learned about it until fairly recently. The American spacecraft Mariner 10 passed by Mercury several times. The first time was in March 1974, and the mission sent back photos and information. Mercury was shown to have craters like the Moon, but virtually no atmosphere. When you arrive, you find it to be a very bleak and desolate planet.

"Boring!" announces VAL as you land. "What a dump." She sniffs. "Perfect place to find one of Carmen's gang, if you ask me."

"What I *am* asking you," you reply, "is if you've actually detected any leads for me to follow."

"Lucky you," she replies, "It appears I have."

If you want to examine:
The Caloris Basin — go to #38
Kuiper — go to #142
Mozart — go to #13 ☞

Kit Incaboodle

Gender: Androgynous
Occupation: Mad-scientist robot
Number of Eyes: Zero
Feature: Tail
Locomotion: Swimming
Favorite Writer: H. G. Wells
Favorite Astronomer: Maria Mitchell
Favorite Food: Liquid hydrogen

Infinity McMath

Gender: Androgynous
Occupation: Certified cosmic accountant
Number of Eyes: One
Feature: Antennae
Locomotion: Bouncing
Favorite Writer: H. G. Wells
Favorite Astronomer: Maria Mitchell
Favorite Food: Toxic waste

Avery Littlebit Phelps

Gender: Male
Occupation: Mascot and apprentice pickpocket
Number of Eyes: Many
Feature: Scales
Locomotion: Flying
Favorite Writer: Arthur C. Clarke
Favorite Astronomer: Maria Mitchell
Favorite Food: Toxic waste

Astro Fizzix

Gender: Androgynous
Occupation: Mad-scientist robot
Number of Eyes: Zero
Feature: Antennae
Locomotion: Walking
Favorite Writer: Arthur C. Clarke
Favorite Astronomer: Maria Mitchell
Favorite Food: Liquid hydrogen

Infinity McMath

Kit Incaboodle

Astro Fizzix

Avery Littlebit Phelps

Bea Miupscotti

Morton U. Bargandfore

Hanover Fist

Carmen Sandiego

Morton U. Bargandfore

Gender: Male
Occupation: Silver-tongued salesman
Number of Eyes: One
Feature: Hair
Locomotion: Slithering
Favorite Writer: H. G. Wells
Favorite Astronomer: Galileo Galilei
Favorite Food: Earth cuisine

Bea Miupscotti

Gender: Female
Occupation: Nightclub entertainer
Number of Eyes: Zero
Feature: Scales
Locomotion: Slithering
Favorite Writer: Ursula Le Guin
Favorite Astronomer: Edwin Hubble
Favorite Food: Earth cuisine

Carmen Sandiego

Gender: Female
Occupation: Intergalactic crime lord
Number of Eyes: Two
Feature: Hair
Locomotion: Walking
Favorite Writer: Ursula Le Guin
Favorite Astronomer: Nicholas Copernicus
Favorite Food: Earth cuisine

Hanover Fist

Gender: Male
Occupation: Spaceship poacher and crackerjack mechanic
Number of Eyes: Many
Feature: Hair
Locomotion: Flying
Favorite Writer: H. G. Wells
Favorite Astronomer: Galileo Galilei
Favorite Food: Toxic waste

MARS

Distance from Sun: 128 to 154 million miles
Diameter of planet: 4,219 miles
Gravity: 0.38 times that of Earth
Atmosphere: Carbon dioxide, nitrogen
Moons: 2
Rotation speed: 24 hours
Length of year: 687 days
Surface Temperature: -60 degrees F

THE OORT CLOUD

The Oort Cloud surrounds the Solar System, and it is where comets originate. If comets are pulled from the cloud, they move toward the Sun. As they approach the Sun, they "grow" tails of particles that make them look like "hairy stars," as they were first called. Some fall into the sun and burn up, while others orbit and the rest are lost in interstellar space.

NEPTUNE

Distance from Sun: 2,793 million miles
Diameter of planet: 30,758 miles
Gravity: 1.2 times that of Earth
Atmosphere: Hydrogen, helium, methane
Moons: 8
Rotation speed: 15.8 hours
Length of year: 165 Earth years
Surface Temperature: -343 degrees F

URANUS

Distance from Sun: 1,783 million miles
Diameter of planet: 32,116 miles
Gravity: 0.8 times that of Earth
Atmosphere: Hydrogen, helium, methane
Moons: 15
Rotation speed: 17.3 hours
Length of year: 84 Earth years
Surface Temperature: -350 degrees F

SUN-SKIMMERS

Sun-skimmers are asteroids that don't stay in the Asteroid Belt. They can come in very close to the Sun and then go far, far out into space. There is a theory that dinosaurs became extinct when a small asteroid hit the Earth in prehistoric times. It must have been a Sun-skimmer, and some scientists think another one could hit the Earth again.

THE ASTEROID BELT

The Asteroid Belt lies between Mars and Jupiter and consists of thousands of chunks of rock. The largest, Ceres, is 600 miles across, but most of them are less than 100 miles across. Over 3,000 have been discovered and named (one after Mr. Spock from "Star Trek"!). Once thought to be the remains of an exploded planet, they are now thought to be "rubbish" left over when a planet didn't form correctly.

METEORS

Meteors are rocks from space that enter the Earth's atmosphere. Many burn up, but some larger ones (called *meteorites*) can survive the impact with the Earth. They seem to be the wreckage from comets, and there are many meteor showers that the Earth passes through every year. They are sometimes called *shooting stars.*

PLUTO

Distance from Sun: 2,743 to 4,572 million miles
Diameter of planet: 1,429 miles
Gravity: 0.05 times that of Earth
Atmosphere: Methane
Moons: 1
Rotation speed: 6.3 days
Length of year: 248 Earth years
Surface Temperature: -382 degrees F

JUPITER

Distance from Sun: 459 to 505 million miles
Diameter of planet: 88,650 miles
Gravity: 2.54 times that of Earth
Atmosphere: Hydrogen, helium, methane
Moons: 16
Rotation speed: 9.84 hours
Length of year: 4,333 days, or 11.86 Earth years
Surface Temperature: 26,637 degrees F

TROJANS AND GREEKS

The Trojans and Greeks are two groups of asteroids that occupy the same orbit as the planet Jupiter. The asteroids in front of Jupiter are named for Greek soldiers in Homer's epic poem *The Iliad*, and the asteroids following Jupiter are the Trojans. Over 200 have been discovered so far.

VENUS

Distance from Sun: 67 million miles
Diameter of planet: 7,521 miles
Gravity: 0.89 times that of Earth
Atmosphere: Carbon dioxide, nitrogen, water
Moons: None
Rotation speed: 243 days
Length of year: 225 days
Surface Temperature: 867 degrees F

MERCURY

Distance from Sun: 28.5 to 43.3 million miles
Diameter of planet: 3,031 miles
Gravity: 0.38 times that of Earth
Atmosphere: Virtually none
Moons: None
Rotation speed: 58.65 days
Length of year: 88 days
Surface Temperature: 800 degrees F

SATURN

Distance from Sun: 835 to 934 million miles
Diameter of planet: 74,565 miles
Gravity: 1.07 times that of Earth
Atmosphere: Hydrogen, helium, ammonia, methane
Moons: 18 (at least)
Rotation speed: 10.25 hours
Length of year: 29.46 Earth years
Surface Temperature: -285 degrees F

TITAN
(MOON OF SATURN)

Distance from Sun: 835 to 934 million miles
Diameter: 3,200 miles
Gravity: 1.6 times that of Earth
Atmosphere: Nitrogen, methane, argon
Moons: None
Rotation speed: 15.9 days
Length of year: 29.46 Earth years
Surface Temperature: -288 degrees F

EARTH

Distance from Sun: 93 million miles
Diameter of planet: 7,926 miles
Gravity: 1
Atmosphere: Nitrogen, oxygen, water, carbon dioxide
Moons: 1
Rotation speed: 24 hours
Length of year: 365 days
Surface Temperature: 60 degrees F

THE EARTH'S MOON

Distance from Sun: 93 million miles
Diameter: 2,160 miles
Gravity: 0.165 times that of Earth
Atmosphere: None
Moons: None
Rotation speed: 27.3 days
Length of year: 27.3 days
Surface Temperature: 0 degrees F

THE GREAT RED SPOT OF JUPITER

The Great Red Spot of Jupiter was first discovered in 1664 by Robert Hooke. It isn't solid, and is most likely a storm that's lasted for hundreds of years! It is 8,400 miles by 18,000 miles in area—more than three times bigger than the Earth.

To investigate this crime: Go to #82

CHARON (THE MOON OF PLUTO)

Charon is the moon of Pluto, the farthest planet in the Solar System. It was discovered in 1978 by James Christy. Not much is known about Charon because it is so far away. It is estimated to be about half as big as Pluto itself.

To investigate this crime: Go to #19

THE ASTEROID ICARUS

An asteroid is like a mini-planet. One of the best-known asteroids is Icarus. Its orbit travels from the Asteroid Belt, which is between Mars and Jupiter, to near the Sun itself—closer even than the planet Mercury. Icarus is named for the mythical Greek youth who made wings and flew too close to the Sun, just like this asteroid.

To investigate this crime: Go to #161

HALLEY'S COMET

Comets are bits of gas and debris left over from the formation of the Solar System. Halley's Comet is the brightest burning of all the comets. Identified in 1682 by Edmund Halley and named after him, it has an orbit that takes 76 years to complete. It was last seen from the Earth in 1986 and will next appear in the year 2062.

To investigate this crime: Go to #134

CHARON
(THE MOON OF PLUTO)

THE GREAT RED SPOT
OF JUPITER

HALLEY'S COMET

THE ASTEROID ICARUS

SCORE CARD 1

Stolen Object:_____

Clues:_____
_____
_____
_____
_____

**Suspect
to arrest:**_____

Move points

Total Move points: _____

Total Game Score: _____

SCORE CARD 2

Stolen Object:_____

Clues: _____
_____
_____
_____
_____

**Suspect
to arrest:**_____

Move points

Total Move points: _____

Total Game Score: _____

SCORE CARD 3

Stolen Object:_____

Clues: _____
_____
_____
_____
_____

**Suspect
to arrest:**_____

Move points

Total Move points: _____

Total Game Score: _____

SCORE CARD 4

Stolen Object:_____

Clues: _____
_____
_____
_____
_____

**Suspect
to arrest:**_____

Move points

Total Move points: _____

Total Game Score: _____

If you think the crook has gone to:
Saturn — go to #54
Neptune — go to #163
Uranus — go to #79

#76. You've reached the planet Mercury, named after the swiftest of the Greek gods. But you're not feeling too swift right now — there's nobody here. Better speed along to #66!

#77. The planet Mars has a day only a few minutes longer than that of the Earth. But you're short a suspect, because there's no one here. Hurry to #66.

#78. Dali Chasma is a valley running through Aphrodite Terra in the southern hemisphere of Venus. You've followed the trail of Avery Littlebit Phelps, but it stops right here. No matter how hard you search, there's not even a little bit of Avery here. Head for #104 to see why.

#79. Uranus is a very pretty shade of blue, but you're feeling a different shade of blue, because there's no sign of the crook you're looking for. Better blast off for #66 instead of staying here.

#80. Mercury is the planet closest to the Sun, but the only thing you're close to is goofing up this case. Better jet on over to #66.

#81. Hektor is a very strange-looking asteroid that's part of the Trojans and Greeks asteroids near the planet Jupiter. It looks at first as if it's shaped like a figure eight. Then you think it might be two rocks actually touching each other. Before you can take a closer look, a tiny flying saucer zips into your ship and lands on the cabin floor. Out of it steps a tiny green alien, about 2 inches tall, who looks up at you and almost falls over backward.

"Take me to your ladder!" the alien cries. "Wow, it's a giant!"

"I'm not so big," you say. "You're just very small."

"Hey, watch it! I'll have you know I'm considered tall where I come from. You must be from the land of the giants, just like that last person I spotted."

That must be the crook you're after. You ask about the thief.

"Odd sort," says the little alien. "Was reading a book called *A Wizard of Earthsea*, by Ursula K. Le Guin. Said something about heading on for a hot spot."

You thank the tiny creature, who jumps into its ship. "Gotta go!" it yells. "I'm short on time."

"And height," you mutter as it zips off. You head back to base at #44 to check out these new clues.

#82. Jupiter is the largest planet in the Solar System. If it had been any larger, it would have turned into a second Sun! As it is, it radiates more heat into space than it gets from the Sun. Jupiter is so big that its volume is 1,330 times the Earth's. Most of that volume is probably liquid hydrogen. Huge floating cloud layers give Jupiter the bands and colors we can see.

As you approach it, VAL gives out a whistle. "Now, that's some planet!" she says. "I'm impressed!"

"I'd be impressed with you," you tell her, "if you came up with something helpful."

"Having a bad hair day?" VAL asks. "Well, as it happens, I *have* come up with some information. The crook visited three of Jupiter's moons and then went on to one of three possible places. If you check out the moons, you might just find a clue or two to help you decide where the thief went."

If you want to check out:
Ganymede — go to #68
Callisto — go to #2
Io — go to #47

If you think the thief went to:
Pluto — go to #89
Saturn — go to #135
Uranus — go to #114

#83. The Earth's Moon is very beautiful — but very dead, too. There's no atmosphere here, so you'll have to be sure your spacesuit is working fine if you want to go for a walk! It's not too hard to get around, because you weigh only a sixth of your weight on Earth. That's one way to lose weight without dieting! Everywhere you look you see craters. Most of them were created by meteors as they hit the Moon.

"Did you know," VAL asks you, "that people were called *lunatics* because it was thought that they were made crazy by the Moon? *Luna* is the old name for the Moon."

"You're a fountain of information," you tell her. "Do you have any that might actually help me on this case?"

"Aside from suggesting that you get your head examined for getting into this business?" she asks. "Yes."

If you want to investigate:
The Sea of Tranquillity — go to #53
Tycho — go to #120
Copernicus — go to #21   ☞

If you think the villain went to:
Uranus — go to #162
Mars — go to #70
Neptune — go to #103

#84. The Sun-skimmer Adonis was discovered in 1936. It sometimes comes within 1.25 million miles of the Earth — almost hitting us, in astronomical terms! At the moment it's a lot farther away, you're happy to discover! As you approach it, you see a small shuttle.

"We come in peace," says its commander. "I'm Captain Kook, of the starship *Booby Prize*."

"Hi," you reply and then ask about the crook you're after.

"Reminds me of all the villains and monsters I've hunted down in my time," he replies. "The Cling-Ons, Harry Thudd, the Roamalongs, the —"

"What about the crook I'm after?" you ask him.

"No, I don't think I've fought that one," he replies. "But I have fought —"

You'd love to stay, but you don't have a million years to spare. As you head back to base at #92, you hear Captain Kook yelling into his communicator: "Spotty! Beam me up! This is mutiny! Beam me up, Spotty!"

#85. Deimos is the outer moon of Mars, and it's quite small — only 10 miles long. Its surface has a lot of small craters on it. As you approach, you see an African-American woman on the tiny moon. Your radio crackles to life.

"Opening hailing frequencies," she calls. "This is Lieutenant Yoohoo-ra."

"Hoorah," you say. Then you ask about the crook you're trailing.

"Somebody did pass by," she tells you. "Reading *The Invisible Man*, by H. G. Wells."

"Did you see him?"

"The invisible man? How could I?" she asks.

"No, the crook!" you reply.

"No, but there was a mention of going to a place with no moons," she tells you.

You thank her and head back to Mars at #106 to check out these leads.

#86. You've reached Tharsis Ridge, which is the main volcanic area of Mars. Luckily, the volcanoes are long dead, as is the trail of Bea Miupscotti. You'd better head for #104.

#87. The methane lake on Saturn's moon Titan is quite pretty but very chilly. You see a man on the banks as you arrive. He waves hello as you approach. In a thick Russian accent, he introduces himself as Mr. Check-Up. You ask him about the crook you're after.

"It was here," he tells you. "It said something about going to a planet that rotates in less than a day."

You thank him for his help and head off back to base at #57 to check up on this information.

#88. You land on Tethys, another strange moon orbiting Saturn. It's one of the "dirty snowball" types that orbit many of the outer planets. It is quite remarkable for having two smaller moons in the same orbit with it, leading them around like a duck with ducklings. There's a huge gash in its off-white surface, called the Ithaca Chasma, which averages 60 miles wide and 3 miles deep.

Lurking in the bottom of the chasm is Astro Fizzix! It's got a pile of snowballs ready, but a snowball fight is not something you're going to let a mad-scientist robot win! Quickly you make your own snowballs. One well-placed shot from you splatters Astro, and some snow gets into its circuits. With a buzz, it shuts down, and you can arrest it. VAL checks Astro's memory banks and find where Pluto's moon, Charon, has been hidden. You've cracked the case more wide open than the chasm has cracked Tethys!

You call the Chief and fill him in.

"Well done!" he exclaims. "The police will take Astro off to the Jailhouse Rock. You head on to the back of the book and see if you've earned that promotion and a bonus!"

#89. You reach Pluto, the outermost planet. "Hello, Pluto," you mutter in your best Mickey Mouse voice. But you're a Mickey Mouse detective — there's nobody here. Head on to #66 pronto!

#90. Atlas is a tiny moon, only a dozen miles across, and is actually inside the famous rings of Saturn! When you come in for a landing, you see a big, scowling being in a yellow uniform. You greet him and ask his name.

"Woof!" he replies, baring big teeth.

"Oh! You don't speak English," you say. "Pity you don't know Poodle!"

"Of course I speak English," he snarls. "My name is Woof!"

You apologize and ask if he's seen the crook you're tailing.

"Yes," he growls. "The miscreant was looking for some Earth cuisine and spoke of going somewhere in orbit near a planet."

You thank him for his information and head back to base at #111 to check out these clues.

#91. You've reached the Trojans and Greeks, a whole bundle of asteroids in the same orbit as Jupiter. You must be in orbit, too, because there's nobody here. Bundle yourself off to #66 immediately!

#92. Sun-skimmers are a special branch of asteroids that don't stay in the Asteroid Belt. Their orbits bring them past the Earth and the other planets as they zip in toward the Sun and then out into space again. It's possible that one day one of these asteroids might hit the Earth!

"Gee," says VAL, "these rocks are almost as big as the ones in your head!"

"When I want to be insulted, I'll let you know," you reply. "Right now, how about giving me a few leads so we can crack this case?"

"No sense of humor," VAL complains. But she does give you what you're after.

If you want to visit:

Apollo — go to #26

Adonis — go to #84

Hermes — go to #129

If you think the crook went to:

Earth — go to #5

Pluto — go to #62

Venus — go to #150

#93. Aristarchus is a very bright crater on a moon of Uranus called Titania. There have been some odd sightings here over the years that may be the venting of radon gas. But that's all there is to see — Astro Fizzix is nowhere to be found. Unless you collect radon gas as a hobby, you'd better zip along to #104.

#94. The Comet Ikeya-Seki, which was formed in the Asteroid Belt, was last seen from the Earth in 1965 and was very bright indeed. You hope it will be as bright for you on the trail of the crook. As you approach it, you see a bright pink spaceship with two girls inside. One has long dark hair; the other, short red hair. Both girls seem very cheerful, and they introduce themselves as Kay and Lily. You ask them about the thief you're searching for.

"We didn't see the person," says red-haired Kay. "We were too busy working on that other comet out there." She points to a small rocky thing not far away.

"But we did pick up a message,' adds Lily. "Something about going to a planet that rotates in less than twelve hours."

At that moment the other comet explodes. The two girls stare at it and then burst into tears. "It's not our fault!" they wail.

You hate to see people cry, so you boost back to your ship at #134 to check out the clue they gave you.

#95. Beta Regio is a region of mountains near the equator of Venus. The only people you find here are a bunch of Girl Scouts selling cookies. You buy a box for your trip back to base at #37. You hope another lead will work out better.

#96. You find yourself heading out to the Asteroid Belt. There are thousands of asteroids out here, but not one sign of the thief you're hunting. Better belt along to #66.

#97. The first asteroid to be discovered was Ceres, on January 1, 1801. It is part of the Asteroid Belt. You've discovered one thing, too — you've made a mistake. Better head on to #66.

#98. Amalthea is a slightly flattened reddish-colored moon. It's very close to Jupiter, and you get a terrific view of the giant planet from here. You discover a unicorn there, of all creatures, and ask him if he's seen the villain you're tailing.

"Yes," he replies. "We went for a walk together. She said that she enjoys watching moons, and will see a few where she goes next."

Thanking him for his help, you head back to Jupiter at #152 to follow up on these clues.

#99. Mercury is one of the hottest places in the Solar System, but your trail is cold. Better beam over to #66 to see why.

#100. Jupiter is known as the king of the planets. You feel like the king of the numbskulls, because there's no sign of the crook you're after. You may as well zoom across to #66.

#101. Maat Mons is a tall mountain right on the Venusian equator. You find a group of furry blue aliens climbing up it. They have long tentacles that they use instead of rope. You ask them if they've seen the crook you're chasing.

"Didn't see anyone," their leader says. "After all, we're mountain*eers*, not mountain *eyes*!" They all laugh like crazy at this. Just what you need — a bunch of furry blue alien comedians. "But we did *hear* something," the leader adds. "Someone saying that Galileo was the greatest, and that the next stop was a place where there was no atmosphere."

Well, that is a help! You wish these furry funnymen luck, then head back to your Cosmohopper at #59 to follow up these clues.

#102. Utopia is a huge, flat plain on the northern part of Mars. It's from a Greek word that means *nowhere*, and that's exactly where you are right now. There's no sign of Kit Incaboodle at all, so you'd better head for #104.

#103. Neptune was named for the Greek god of the sea. It's not hard to see why — the planet is a blue-green color, just like the ocean on a nice day. It's a large planet, though its solid, rocky core may be only the size of the Earth. Over this is an ocean about 5,000 miles deep, made from water and ammonia. Its atmosphere is mostly hydrogen, but there are clouds of ammonia in the dark sky.

"With all that ammonia," VAL jokes, "even one of Carmen's gang could come clean."

"I'll handle the jokes around here," you tell VAL. "You just come up with some information to help me clean up the case."

"I'd better find you a good joke book, too," she complains. But she does have some leads for you.

If you want to check out:
Triton — go to #145
Nereid — go to #16
Proteus — go to #41

If you think the crook has fled to:
Titan — go to #57
The Trojans and Greeks — go to #91
Saturn — go to #124

#104. Well, you've reached the right place, but you've tried to arrest the wrong suspect! You must have messed up or missed some of the clues. You'd better head for the back of the book to see how you've done, but add another 10 points to your travel points for making such a bad mistake. Next time, be more careful in reading the clues!

#105. Hyperion is a rocky little moon of Saturn that isn't quite round. It looks like a passing asteroid may have knocked a huge chunk out of it. You're glad that happened a long time ago! It would be nasty to be on the receiving end of such a punch. But you haven't caught anything — especially not Infinity McMath, who isn't here. Better beam on over to #104 to see why.

#106. Mars is smaller than Planet Earth, but its day is almost exactly the same length. It even has polar ice caps. But that's about as close to your home planet as it gets, because Mars has no oceans or rivers anymore. Now it's just covered with dried-up riverbeds and reddish dust, which sometimes creates huge dust storms.

"I thought Mars was supposed to be covered in chocolate," you joke.

"That's a Mars bar," VAL replies with a sigh.

"A Mars bar?" you ask. "Isn't that where you go for a drink after work on this planet?"

"Fortunately," she says, "I've got some clues for you to check up on. Hopefully, you'll be too busy to make up any more terrible jokes."

If you want to investigate:
Phobos — go to #31
Deimos — go to #85
Olympus Mons — go to #122

If you think the thief went to:
Titan — go to #18
Venus — go to #59
Earth — go to #143

#107. Titan is one of the biggest moons in the Solar System, and orbits Saturn. And you've made one of your biggest mistakes, because there's no sign of the thief here. Blast off for #66!

#108. Rhea and Thea are two tall mountains in Beta Regio, just north of Venus's equator. You'd better go to the rhea — er, *rear* — of the class, because there's no sign of Infinity McMath here. Zip over to #104 and you'll find out why.

#109. You see Titan, a moon of Saturn just ahead of you. It's a huge moon whose surface has never been seen from the Earth, or even when photographed from a spacecraft. That's because there's a thick orange-colored cloud layer over the whole moon. Instead of water, though, the cloud is composed mostly of nitrogen!

"Well, gumshoe," VAL tells you, "it looks like you lucked out again. According to my sensors, the crook we're after is down there somewhere." She can't be certain where, because of all those clouds.

If you think the villain's hiding near:
The methane sea — go to #113
The methane waterfall — go to #9
The methane ice cups — go to #146

#110. Peary is a crater on the north pole of the Earth's Moon. That's appropriate, because it's named after an explorer of the Earth's North Pole. You're up a pole, though, because Kit Incaboodle isn't here. Shoot over to #104 to see why.

#111. Saturn is the second-largest planet in the Solar System, and it is completely unmistakable because of the beautiful rings around it. Jupiter, Uranus, and Neptune all have rings, too, but they're very faint — not at all like Saturn's glorious bands. At first glance, it looks as if there are two rings, separated by a dark band of empty space, but this isn't quite the case.

Speaking of cases, you remember you're on one, and not here to play tourist. "Got anything for me to go on?" you ask VAL.

"I wish you'd go on without me so I can get some rest," VAL grumbles. "But I've scanned the planet and come up with three places the crook stopped off and three places the thief might have fled to."

If you want to look into:
The rings — go to #7
Atlas — go to #90
The shepherd moons — go to #115

If you think the crook moved to:
The Trojans and Greeks — go to #44
The Asteroid Belt — go to # 69
Titan — go to #107

#112. Ceres was one of the first asteroids to be discovered. It's also the largest, at just over 600 miles across. You begin to look around, you see a furry brown alien approaching.

"Yo!" it calls out. "Welcome to my asteroid.

I'm ELF."

"ELF?" you ask, puzzled.

"Yup — it stands for Extremely Lovable Furball." The alien laughs and then burps loudly. You wonder why it thinks it's lovable. "See this?" it asks, pointing to the asteroid it's standing on. "This is Ceres. And that smaller one over there is mini-Ceres. Mini-series? Get it?" ELF laughs again. "Ha! I just kill myself."

"That saves me the trouble," you reply. You ask about the crook you're looking for.

"Yeah, yeah, yeah," ELF mutters. "I saw something. The crook mentioned going to a place orbiting a planet somewhere. I wasn't paying attention. I was waiting for my pizza delivery. You haven't seen it yet, have you?"

You tell the alien you haven't, then zip back to base at #161 before it tries another terrible puns.

#113. You arrive on the shore of the methane sea of Saturn's moon Titan. It looks deserted. There's a big sign up: NO SWIMMING. You look at the sea — there are huge chunks of methane ice in it. There's no chance you'd even *think* of going for a swim in that! With a shudder, you head back to your Cosmohopper at #109 to try a different lead.

#114. Uranus is a large planet whose surface is hidden below thick clouds. The strangest thing about Uranus is the way it rotates. Most planets, such as the Earth, rotate like a top, but Uranus looks more like a ball rolling around in its orbit! It has rings, too, though they aren't as bright or pretty as those of Saturn. Some of these rings are only about 60 feet across, and they're probably the remains of a moon that was torn apart by gravity!

VAL scans the planet as you approach, and then she says, "Well, it looks like the crook was here but fled. Still, he, she, or it did stop off in three places. Maybe you can get a clue where to go from them."

If you want to check out:
Miranda — go to #126
Umbriel — go to #55
The rings — go to #23

If you think the villain went to:
Meteors — go to #168
The asteroids — go to #97
Mercury — go to #39

#115. The shepherd moons of Saturn are Atlas, Prometheus, and Pandora. They are called *shepherd moons* because they seem to guide the path and formation of Saturn's innermost rings, like a shepherd guides and gathers sheep. You fly over all three moons, but the only thing you find is a take-out menu from a Chinese restaurant on Earth. Then you head back to base at #111 to check this out.

#116. Titania, the largest moon of Uranus, was discovered by Sir William Herschel just six years after he discovered the planet itself. It's made up mostly of ice, which is cracked and cratered by all the battering it received. You find an alien creature that looks like a beachball with lots of eyes and legs, skating about on the surface.

"I'm practicing for the next Olympics," it tells you.

You ask about the crook you'd like to put on ice.

"Yeah, that nasty thing was here," it replies. "Said this was too cold, and aimed to go closer to the Sun than the Earth is. Even drank all my spare liquid hydrogen!"

"Thanks," you tell it. "See you later, skater." Then you head back to your Cosmohopper at #29 to check out these clues.

#117. Neptune has two main rings and a fainter one inside both of those. They're not as colorful or spectacular as the rings of Saturn. As you approach a ring, you find a small jeweler's shop.

There's a bright yellow birdlike creature in the store. "May I interest you in a ring?" the creature asks.

"No," you answer. "But how about some information on a crook whose neck I'd like to wring?"

"Sorry," says the big bird. "You won't get me to sing. I'm no stool pigeon."

"Later for you," you say, then head back to Neptune at #163 to try another lead — you hope with better luck.

#118. The Sea of Serenity is where the last Apollo capsule landed on the Earth's Moon, in December 1972. Since then, the whole Moon has been peaceful — till Carmen Sandiego and her gang got to work! As you arrive, you see a bearlike being sitting cross-legged on the sea, deep in meditation. You walk over and see that it's a Yoga bear. Beside the spaced-out being is a piece of paper, which you look at. Then you look again — it's a list of the addresses where each one of Carmen's gang is hiding out!

If you're going to arrest:

Avery Littlebit Phelps — go to #6

Morton U. Bargandfore — go to #72

Infinity McMath — go to #130

Astro Fizzix — go to #93

Bea Miupscotti — go to #151

☞

#119. Sinope is the outermost of Jupiter's moons — and only 22 miles across. It was discovered in 1914. There's nobody there when you arrive, but you do find footprints left in the dust by the crook you're after. Then you head back to Jupiter at #152 to check this out.

#120. Tycho, a crater that's 55 miles across, has bright rays extending from it. As seen from the Earth, it's one of the brightest craters on the Moon. You discover a neon-orange-colored alien in the crater, selling balloons!

You ask the creature about the crook you're chasing.

"The one that thinks Maria Mitchell is the greatest?" it asks you. "Said something about going to a place where there was plenty of helium to refill the balloons the crook bought from me."

You thank the alien and buy one of its balloons before heading back to your Cosmohopper at #83 to check out these clues.

#121. Enceladus is quite an active moon of Saturn. Water under its icy layer creeps up to the surface to repair the damage made by meteor strikes. Nothing can repair the damage you've made, though — Hanover Fist isn't here. Better blast off for #104 to find out why.

#122. Olympus Mons — Mount Olympus — is a huge volcano on Mars. It is 15 miles high, and the biggest mountain anywhere in the Solar System, it is truly a sight not to be missed. You find a book that the thief dropped here — *The War of the Worlds*, by H. G. Wells. On the bookmark is written: "Somewhere with no moons next." You hurry back to your ship at #106 to follow up on these clues.

#123. The Encke Comet was first spotted in 1818, and it returns to Earth about every three and a third years. You check it out, but there's nothing to be seen out of the ordinary. You head back to the Oort Cloud at #134 and hope that the other leads will be better.

#124. You've reached Saturn, with its famous rings. As you look at them, your phone rings. It's the Chief, telling you to head straight to #66!

#125. In one of Pluto's icy seas, you see an iceberg made of frozen methane. On it is an alien creature that's bright blue, holding a fishing rod. "Caught anything?" you ask it.

"Only a cold," it replies with a sneeze. You ask about the crook you're tailing, and the alien nods between sneezes. "Was here," it sniffs. "Said it was too cold, and was going closer to the Sun than the Earth."

You thank the alien and wish it luck before heading back to your Cosmohopper at #19 to check out this chilly clue.

#126. Miranda is the smallest of Uranus's five main moons, with some very odd surface features caused by the planet's gravity. There are parallel cracks and valleys, collapsed mountains, and wild-looking ridges. It's a strange sight indeed. As you search for the place where the crook landed, you spot a discarded lunchbag. Inside it is a half-finished Tupperware container of toxic waste. The thief must have been in a hurry, not even finishing lunch! You hurry back to Uranus at #114 to check out this lead.

#127. The Valles Marineris is a huge gash in the surface of Mars just south of the equator. It runs for over 3,000 miles. And speaking of running, you spot Carmen Sandiego herself running for her spaceship! Thinking fast, you bring your Cosmohopper down low between her and her ship, using your jets to blow lots of dust into the thin air. This stops Carmen from finding her ship and making her getaway. Then you have VAL use her sensors to detect Carmen. You slap on the handcuffs with a grin.

"You're Carmen with me to jail," you tell her. Then you call up the Chief to tell him that you've caught Carmen and discovered where she's hidden Halley's Comet.

"Excellent work!" the Chief exclaims. "The police will take her along to the Jailhouse Rock. You get yourself to the back of the book and see if you've earned yourself a bonus and a promotion for this great piece of detecting!"

#128. The ice continent on the Saturn's moon Titan is a huge area made up of solidified water surrounded by methane seas. It's very impressive, but there's no sign of anyone here. You head on back to base at #57 to try another lead, hoping for better luck.

#129. Hermes was one of the first Sun-skimmers to be discovered. It passed within half a million miles of the Earth in 1937. What a close call! You land near an alien that looks like a big blue chicken wearing headphones. Then you realize that it *is* wearing headphones — and listening to some awful music! You ask about the crook you're hunting.

"Hey, man, that rascal was here," the blue bird tells you. "Said something about heading for a planet with one moon — do you dig?"

You dig it, and you thank *it*. The alien returns to its music. You go back to #92 to check out this lead.

#130. Kepler is a 20-mile-wide crater on the Earth's Moon. It has bright material (called *rays*) streaming from it. You don't feel too bright yourself, though, because there's no sign of Infinity McMath here at all. With a sigh, you blast off for #104.

#131. You've reached Saturn — which is a shame, because the crook you're after hasn't. Better zoom over to #66 to find out why.

#132. The Helen Planita is a large plain on the Planet Venus. It is named after Helen of Troy, who is supposed to have been the most beautiful woman who ever lived. You may as well enjoy the view, because there's no sign of Morton U. Bargandfore here. Better lift off for #104.

#133. The Dead Sea in Israel is the lowest lake on Earth, at 1,300 feet below sea level. It's called the Dead Sea because it's so salty that nothing can live in it. If you swim in it, you have no trouble floating, but you don't want to swallow any water! Finding a swimmer there now, you ask if she's seen the crook you're looking for.

"The robot?" she asks. "Yes, it was here. Said it hated salt water and was going where it could swim in methane. Imagine!"

Thanking her for her help, you head back to your Cosmohopper at #5 to check out this clue.

#134. The Oort Cloud lies far beyond the planets of the Solar System. It is where the rocks and ice that make up the comets are formed. Then the comets are tugged out of the cloud by the gravitational pull of the Sun and the planets, and they start a long journey into the main part of the Solar System. Some of them will plunge to a fiery death in the Sun. Others will fly right through the Solar System and on into space, lost forever. But others will get caught by gravity and start to orbit the Sun at regular intervals.

"Well," VAL says, "when you've finished sleeping, I've got some information for you."

"I wasn't sleeping," you tell her. "I was *thinking*."

"Hard to tell the difference with you," VAL replies. "Now, here's what I've found: The crook stopped off at three places, then went on to one of three destinations. If you check out the places, you might find clues telling you where the thief went."

If you want to investigate:

The Comet Ikeya-Seki — go to #94
The Encke Comet — go to #123
The West Comet — go to #36

If you think that the crook went to:

Uranus — go to #160
Jupiter — go to #48
Saturn — go to #111

#135. You're in orbit around Saturn, but aside from the moons and the rings, there's nothing to see. Better head off to #66.

#136. Slipher is a fairly large crater in the southern hemisphere of Mars, near the Argyre Plain. There's a big silver-colored man there, and you ask him about the crook you're trailing.

"Sorry," the Slipher Man says in a metallic voice. "Haven't seen anyone but you for days."

You thank him for his help and head back to your ship at #60 to try one of the other leads.

#137. Until the first spacecraft visited it, not much could be seen on Mercury. There's not much for you either, so boost your rockets over to #66.

#138. Phoebe is the moon farthest from Saturn, and you're as far as you can get from catching Morton U. Bargandfore. Shoot over to #104.

#139. The Earth is a pretty planet from space — all blue and white. You're pretty blue right now, and not quite right. Head over to #66 and you'll see why.

#140. Haystack Valley forms a deep gash

in Mercury's surface, running north from the equator. You find a small alien creature that looks like a pink mole burrowing away there. It pops out of its hole and grins at you. You ask it about the thief you're seeking.

"She was here," the mole replies. "I'm a prospector, and she tried to steal my samples. The nerve! I told her where to go. Somewhere with lots of moons, that's where she was heading."

You thank the little creature, who returns to its digging, while you return to your ship at #73 to follow up on this information.

#141. The Atalanta Plain is a low, flat area in the north of Venus. There's no sign of Hanover Fist, just a tourist from Arkansas, wearing Levi's and whistling "Venus in Blue Jeans." Better leave the traveler and head for #104.

#142. Kuiper is a bright crater on the planet Mercury. It is 25 miles in diameter, named for the American astronomer Gerard Kuiper. You find a greenish alien in a shell practicing with *nunchucks*. It's obviously a Teenage Militant Nunchuck Turtle. You ask it about the villain you're after.

"Check it out, dude," the alien replies. "That nefarious nasty was here. Said something about below zero or colder. Talk about delivering frozen pizzas, man!"

You thank the alien for its help and leave it to its workout. You've got your work cut out for you — and return to your ship at #75 to check out this clue.

#143. The Earth is home for billions of living creatures — and not one of them is the crook you're seeking. Better boost on over to #66!

#144. Arcadia is a vast plain in the Martian north. You can see for miles here, almost to infinity — but not to Infinity McMath. There's no sign of him at all. Zip along to #104 and see why.

#145. Triton is Neptune's largest moon and is (astronomically speaking) very close to the planet. In a million years or so, it may get so close that gravity will pull it part and make it into rings. You've got plenty of time to land and check it out first, though!

There's a small methane sea, and in it you find seven mermaids. "We are the daughters of Triton," they tell you. You say hello and ask about the villain you're chasing.

"The crook was here, trying to steal our methane," the oldest daughter tells you.

"We chased the crook away," the second adds. "I'm sure I heard something about going on to a place that has lots of methane."

You thank them and head back to Neptune at #103 to check out this new clue.

#146. You arrive at the methane ice caps of Saturn's moon Titan and find a ski resort for all sorts of aliens. You stop at the First Aid Station and ask one of the ice cap aides if anyone has seen the crook you're chasing.

"No," she tells you. "But the crook's assistant is here." She points to an alien creature in bed with four broken legs. "Tripped over its own feet while skiing," the aide explains. "Broke four legs."

The villain's fast asleep, but you see on one of the casts that the crook you're looking for has written his address — and those of the other members of the gang!

If the villain you're tracking is:

Bea Miupscotti — go to #30

Hanover Fist — go to #121

Astro Fizzix — go to #88

Carmen Sandiego — go to #158

Kit Incaboodle — go to #42

Infinity McMath — go to #105

Morton U. Bargandfore — go to #138

Avery Littlebit Phelps — go to #67

Avery Littlebit Phelps — go to #67

#147. The Leonids are a meteor shower best seen from Earth on November 17, in the constellation Leo. They are the wreckage from the comet Temple-Tuttle. When you arrive, you find an alien creature in the meteor shower, a being shaped like a hairy green football. You ask it about the crook you're tracking.

"Wait until I get out of the shower," it grumbles. As it towels off, it says, "The villain you're after was here and spoke about going somewhere that has a twenty-four-hour day."

You thank it for its help.

"Never fails," the creature grumbles. "Someone always calls when I'm in the shower."

You head back to base at #168 to check out this clue.

#148. Neptune was named for the Roman water god, and you're feeling all wet right now. There's no sign of your quarry, so hurry on to #66.

#149. Oberon is a large moon, the farthest out from Uranus. Like most moons, it is littered with craters. You find an ugly alien creature there, with large ears and pointy teeth. "I'm Quirk," it tells you. "What do you want?"

You ask about the crook you're trailing.

"That thief!" says Quirk. "Stole a six-pack of liquid hydrogen from me! And complained because I was out of nitrogen."

As Quirk goes on grumbling, you head back to Uranus at #29 to check on these clues.

#150. Venus is named for the Roman goddess of love, but you're not in love right now. There's no sign of the villain you're hunting, so you'd better lift off for #66.

#151. You've trailed Bea Miupscotti to the crater Archimedes. It's a very old crater and has been partly filled in by lava flows. There's no sign of Bea here, so you'd better flow along to #104.

#152. Jupiter, the largest planet in the Solar System, makes an extremely impressive sight as you approach it. It's made up almost entirely of liquid hydrogen, but the brightly colored clouds above this hydrogen sea are mostly ammonia. The colors are bright reds and oranges, and faint browns. The famous Great Red Spot is a huge, whirling storm, but there are plenty of other swirling patterns all over the clouds.

"Way cool," says VAL. "Well, are you going

to sit and stare at the sights all day, or are you willing to do a little work? I've whipped up some information for you."

If you want to check out:
Europa — go to #24
Amalthea — go to #98
Sinope — go to #119

If you think the crook went to:
Titan — go to #3
Mars — go to #60
Neptune — go to #148

#153. Aphrodite Terra is the large southern continent on Venus. It contains huge mountains as well as the deepest valley on the planet. But there's no sign of the crook you're tracking here, so you head back to your Cosmohopper at #37 to try a different lead.

#154. Mercury is ahead of you, and that's as ahead as you'll get here. The trail is cold, so head for #66.

#155. The Freyja Mountes are the northernmost chain of mountains on Venus. The mountains are tall and craggy and look like they'd be difficult to climb. Plus, the atmosphere here is so thick that it's impossible to see through it. But you find the alien mountaineer and ask about the thief you're seeking.

"Saw the villain," the climber tells you. "Spoke about going on to a place with no atmosphere. Can't say I blame the crook — this fog is a bit thick. Well, I must be off."

"You must be," you say as the alien disappears into the fog. What an airhead! You leave it to its climbing and head back to your ship at #59 to check out this clue.

#156. The crater's Bond — just Bond. It's north of Mars's Argyre Plain, and you find a brass band practicing there: the Bond Band. You ask the leader about the crook you're seeking, but the band's so loud that he can't hear you. You can't stand the noise any longer, so you head back to base at #60 and hope one of the other leads is better — and quieter!

#157. Neptune is sometimes the planet farthest from the Sun, since Pluto has a very odd orbit. And you're as far as you can get from solving the case. Zip along to #66 and discover why.

#158. You're alone on Dione, the darkest of Saturn's moons. Things are dark for you, too, because there's no sign of Carmen Sandiego here. Better head on to #104 to be enlightened.

#159. Fra Mauro is a crater near the equator of Earth's Moon. It is where Apollo 14 landed. You find a small gray alien creature there, sweeping away. As you approach, it looks up.

"Can't stop and chat," it tells you. "Lots to do. Look at all this rubbish those astronauts left behind! You'd better clean up after yourself before you go!"

What a grouch! You beat a hasty retreat to your Cosmohopper at #14 and hope that one of the other leads is in a better mood.

#160. Uranus was the first planet to be discovered by modern astronomers. You discover that it's the wrong place to be, though. Head for #66 instead.

#161. The Asteroid Belt lies between the planets Mars and Jupiter. There are thousands and thousands of asteroids that make up this area. Most of them are very small, but some are over a hundred miles across. It was once thought that they were the wreckage left after a planet exploded, but nowadays it is thought that they were always just rocks. There are other asteroids that have been tugged out of this region by gravity. Some of the moons of the planets might even be asteroids that have been pulled out of place and into orbit around Jupiter, Mars, and Saturn.

VAL finishes her scanning. "Well," she tells you, "you're in luck. I've managed to discover three asteroids that the thief stopped off at while making a getaway. There are three possible places the crook could have gone on to. If you check out the asteroids, maybe you'll be able to find some clues as to which destination is correct."

If you want to look over:
Ceres — go to #112
Vesta — go to #170
Pallas — go to #8

If you think that the crook went to:
Titan — go to #49
Mercury — go to #137
The Moon — go to #83

#162. Uranus is a pretty-looking blue-green world. Unless you want to stop and stare, you'd better blast off for #66, though.

#163. Neptune was actually first spotted by Galileo in 1612, but he didn't realize it was a new planet, so it remained virtually undiscovered. In 1845 its existence was predicted separately by Leverrier in France and Adams in England, and it was then found the following year. Neptune is a deep blue color, with bright white methane ice clouds in the atmosphere, as well as huge, dark storms that rage for decades or centuries.

VAL finishes her work and whistles loudly to get your attention. "What do you think this is?" she asks. "A sight-seeing tour? You're here to work, and you'd better get busy on the clues I've found for you!"

If you want to investigate:
The Great Dark Spot — go to #22
The rings — go to #117
The ammonia sea — go to #1

If you think that the crook went to:
Mercury — go to #154
The Asteroid Belt — go to #50
The Sun-skimmers — go to #92

#164. Just as on Earth, there's a range of mountains on the Moon called the Alps. You've trailed Carmen Sandiego to the Lunar Alps, but you need some help, because she's not here. Lift off for #104.

#165. Patroclus is named after a Greek warrior and it's part of the Trojan and Greek asteroids near Jupiter. A spy in the enemy camp! When you land, you find a golden-skinned android that introduces itself as Ditto.

"Same to you," you say, then ask it about the crook you're trailing.

"The one that enjoys Ursula K. Le Guin?" Ditto asks. "The thief spoke about going on to a low-gravity planet."

You thank the android for its help and head back to base at #44 to check out these clues.

#166. The Navka Plain is just on the equator of Venus, and there's one thing immediately plain to you — Kit Incaboodle is just up ahead! Because Kit's so lazy, it doesn't even try to get away. You drop a net over it and scoop it into your ship. Then you call the Chief to tell him you've cracked the case, bagged Kit Incaboodle, and discovered where Icarus has been hidden.

"Way to go," the Chief says happily. "We'll

see to it that Kit does a long stretch on the Jailhouse Rock. Meanwhile you head to the back of the book and see if you've earned that bonus and promotion!"

#167. You reach Venus, but the cloud-covered planet leaves you in the dark. Better jet over to #66 to find out what's happening.

#168. Meteors are often visible in the night sky as they burn up while entering the Earth's atmosphere. They are often called *shooting stars* because they look like stars falling to Earth. In space they are known as meteoroids, and if they survive their fiery trip to Earth, the remains are called meteorites. These pieces of rock have bombarded all the planets and moons of the Solar System. The force of their impact caused the craters we see on these worlds. There are meteorite craters on Earth, too, such as the Barringer Crater in Arizona.

"Rock and roll," says VAL. "Those are the rocks, and I'm on a roll. I've come up with some fresh clues for you."

"Wonderful," you reply. "Hit me with them."

If you want to look into:

The Perseids — go to #63
The Leonids — go to #147
The Orionids — go to #10

If you think that the crook fled to:
Earth — go to #27
Mars — go to #106
Mercury — go to #80

#169. Mount Elysium is a sharp peak rising from the Elysium Plain on Mars, and you've tracked Astro Fizzix here. But the trail is cold, so look sharp and head to #104.

#170. Vesta is the third-largest asteroid in the Asteroid Belt. On it you find a young woman typing away like crazy. "I'm a science fiction writer," she tells you. "This is a great place for ideas. My name is Esther."

You ask Esther from Vesta if she spotted the crook you're chasing.

"Yes," she tells you. "The thief interrupted my work, then spoke about going somewhere that orbits a planet."

You thank her for her help, then head back to base at #161 to check out this clue.

SCORING CHART

Add up all your travel points (you did remember to mark 1 point for each time you moved to a new number, didn't you?). If you have penalty points for trying to arrest the wrong person, add those in, too. Then check your score against the chart below to see how you did.

0 – 17:
You can't really have solved these cases in so few steps. Either you're bragging about your abilities, or you're actually working with Carmen's gang. Be honest and try again — if you dare!

18 – 40:
All right, super sleuth! You work very well and don't waste time (or space). Very well done indeed. You deserve your promotion and the nice bonus you'll receive in your next paycheck!

41 – 60:

Private eye material! You're a good, steady worker, and you get your man, or woman, or thing! Still, you've got a little room for improvement, so maybe you'd like to try another case and see if you can get that promotion!

61 – 80:

Detective first class! You're not a world-famous private eye yet, but you're getting there. Try another case and see if you can move up a grade or two.

81 – 100:

Rookie material. You're taking too long to track down the crooks. Next time they're going to get away from you. Try a little harder on the next case and see if you can do better than this.

Over 100:

Are you sure you're cut out to be a detective? You're acting more like a space cadet! Still, if you think you're really detective material, why not try again? This might just have been a bad day for you. Better luck next time!